There are lots of hens on Moat Farm. Every morning, Farmer Green feeds them with corn.

This is Hetty.

She is sitting on her nest.

From her nest she can see the sacks of corn in the barn.

She crosses to the barn and looks around. Ben and Neb are asleep in the sun.

Hetty starts to peck at some corn that has spilled out of a sack.

Molly the cat and her kitten, Tolly, are looking around the barnyard.

They stop at the barn and sniff. They can smell something interesting.

They pad into the barn and creep along. Tolly stops and sniffs at the sack of corn.

Then he pats the sack. In the sack, Hetty feels afraid. She sits as still as she can.

Just then, there is a scratching sound. Molly and Tolly look round, and see rats!

They dash to the corner of the barn and the rats run off.

Lucky Hetty slips quickly back to the hen house and her nest and eggs.